BITES EYES

ALSO BY MATTHEW R. DAVIS

Supermassive Black Mass

If Only Tonight We Could Sleep

Midnight in the Chapel of Love

The Dark Matter of Natasha

BITES EYES

13 MACABRE MORSELS

MATTHEW R. DAVIS

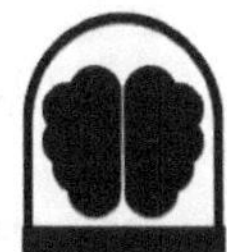

Brain Jar Press
PO Box 6687
Upper Mt Gravatt, QLD, 4122
Australia
www.BrainJarPress.com

Cover design by Peter Ball
Cover Image: Alien Eye Creature, Transposeimages/Shutterstock

ISBN: 978-1-922479-81-5 (Ebook) | 978-1-922479-82-2 (Chapbook)

CONTENTS

YOU'VE SEEN THE BUTCHER

The scariest person you know? The last person you'd want to find standing over your bed?

Libby Butcher.

She works with you in the supermarket deli department, and you don't know if the name's a coincidence or an inspiration. She's *creepy*, man. Pale blue eyes, arms like a stevedore, laugh like a bone saw. First time you heard that laugh, one of the deli girls found a lump of jelly on her shoulder with a pupil in it and screamed. "Just keeping an eye on you," Butcher said. Cue bone saw.

This stockboy, Marko, he'll sleep with anything. Said he chatted her up once on a dare, went home with her. Said her place was chilly as a coldroom and all the fixtures were brushed steel. Said there's not a single hair on her entire body and her pussy smelled like freshly sliced fritz. Said he doesn't know if she bit him because she came or the other way around. He's avoided the deli ever since.

When she watches you work, she smiles like she's sizing you up for prime cuts. She was born for the abattoir — looks like she'd be right at home with a captive bolt pistol and rib shears. You can imagine her a thousand years ago dressed in furs and raw guts, tearing the skins off deer with her bare hands.

You've never seen her eat a vegetable. Just cold collations, all meat all the time. You'd believe it if you heard she licked the benches and gutters clean after every shift. This week, she's been bringing in her own German sausages for lunch.

Thing is, Hans from the bakery section went missing last week. Big boy he was, lots of meat on those bones. Everyone's wondering where he's gone.

You can't help thinking the wurst.

CHRISTMAS PRESENCE

"What's that smell?"

Erin turned from the stove and beamed over at the table, where Kym sat kicking his little feet in impatience. He fairly glowed in the morning sun, so vital, so beautiful. How had she ever lived without him?

"Mummy's making Christmas breakfast, honey. And then... *presents*!"

"Awesome!"

Erin poked at the eggs. They bubbled and spat and smoked, and they smelled like burning flesh. And now David's lips pressed against the back of her head.

"Morning, darling!" She wouldn't have thought her smile could get any bigger, but it did; with her boys, every Christmas was the best Christmas yet. "Love you."

Her husband's voice was low, sad. "Why do you keep doing this to yourself, Erin?"

"Doing what?"

She turned, distressed. David was frowning, and not at the ugly dark stains seeping through his business shirt. His hair was on fire.

"You know," he said.

Erin couldn't bear to look, to see him that way. She stared down at the eggs as they blurred into a misshapen mass like melting skin.

"I know," she whispered, and closed her eyes to seal in the sting of tears.

When she opened them, the kitchen was cloaked in night's shadows. She only knew where she was because the shape of this room was as familiar as David's touch; now it was empty, barren, the floorboards coated in the dust that clogged her rank, tangled hair. She still held the frying pan, but it was so small, a child's plaything, and the tiny plastic stove provided no heat from its painted-on rings. She knelt on the floor, muttering to herself about a world long gone — alone, insane.

But *not* alone.

Voices outside the front door.

People! — *strangers*.

Erin glanced over to the corner where she slept now. A ratty old mattress sat there, dirty blanket atop it like a disarrayed shroud, lumped and heavy like someone already lay waiting beneath it. She could be out of sight in seconds; maybe the strangers would come and go without ever knowing she was here.

But so soon, the front door popped open. Erin cringed into herself as two tipsy teens stumbled into her house, staring about in nervous excitement.

"Chill, baby," the boy said. "No-one lives here. The owner and his kid died in a car crash last year — his wife flipped out and vanished."

"So sad." The girl's face screwed up. "What's that smell?"

The pair exchanged a sickly glance and walked in, one accidentally kicking over the playset stove. Neither noticed Erin crouched beside them, but she fought off understanding as they moaned, covered their noses, pointed trembling fingers at the lumpy blanket in the corner.

Why do you keep doing this to yourself, Erin?

She squeezed her eyes shut and wished the night away, and when she opened them, Kym was kicking his feet impatiently at the breakfast table, and David kissed the back of her head, and Erin knew this Christmas was going to be the best Christmas yet.

COLOURS THAT FLICKER IN WATER

When Claire slips through the back door, announced by the security-conscious jingle of an old shop bell, it's late but none of her housemates are home. That suits her just fine. She wants to kick back upstairs and listen to a strange LP she'd found at the op shop today. She'd felt compelled to buy it because one of the songs bears her name.

She slips the record out of its sleeve and filmy bag. It's an unusual misty grey colour, but there must have been subtle highlights in it, for as she places the LP on her turntable, little flecks of brilliance flash in her bedroom's light. The effect is similar to rubbing her eyes too hard, like glimpsing colours that flicker in water beneath a city bridge at night.

Claire slips on her headphones, drops the needle. "Tonight" begins as she sits on the floor to peruse the record sleeve. The cover shares the gloomy shade of the record, perhaps a picture of fog or a poorly developed photograph. No credits, just the band name: The Dead Beat. There's a group picture on the inner sleeve, as indistinct as the cover — three tall, thin figures with long white fingers, blurry faces, teased black manes. The music sounds as empty as the images.

A cold, disquieting guitar rings out over slow, savage beats and sliver-of-ice bass, the baritone vocal drenched in sepulchral reverb. Not bad for one pound, even if she's never heard of them before.

The songs march on, each as moribund and chilly as the last: "When You're Alone", "The Dead Are Coming". Claire shivers as a dank requiem called "For You" ends the first side and gets up on her knees to flip the record. She can't wait to share this album with her housemates — its cold, stark brilliance.

As the second side begins, she lights a cigarette and pushes the window up, relishing the cool breath of the breeze. Flicking ash into the garden below, Claire pauses and frowns, staring down into the shadows. For a moment, she can believe she's seen something tall and thin flickering in the corner of her eye.

The record is getting to her, that's all — a testament to its power. She tells herself that, but the next time she leans out, she thinks she sees another shape sliding swiftly out of sight. Both shadows resembled the wraiths in The Dead Beat's sleeve picture. She knows plenty of guys and girls who do themselves up like that. Is someone playing a daft joke?

Claire butts out her smoke and closes the window to mollify her paranoia. A self-titled track begins Side B, followed by "At Your Door"; these numbers could have been funeral dirges for a dead poet, pounded out in a mist-shrouded graveyard by skull-faced punks. Appropriately, the third and penultimate song is called "Lose Yourself in Us", something Claire cannot fail to do. Why are these guys not huge? Granted, they've as much pop appeal as a corpse falling out of its coffin, but among her kind, bands like this are gods — their names venerated and carved into willing skin, their music echoing through tomb-like minds to ease the suffering of another slow-death day.

Finally, her song: "Claire". She sits back and closes her eyes, lost in the chilling chime of guitar harmonics, as the singer simply intones one syllable over and over: *"Claire/Claire/Claire/Claire."* Her name seems to lose all meaning, becomes a random sound in his mouth, an echo that has long since lost any relation to its source. The song slouches on for what feels like an age, finally fading out into stark silence as a distant thud, mixed far in the background, continues the snare beat as a hollow coda.

Claire opens her eyes, the spell wearing off, and reaches for her cigarettes. That's when she notices two things: the swift curls of mist gathering outside her bedroom window, and the stylus of her turntable caught in the run-out groove of the LP. The record is over.

The distant beat continues.

Ripping her headphones off, Claire realises it's coming from downstairs. Has one of her housemates locked themselves out? If so, they've found their key, for now she hears the shop bell jingle as the door bursts open.

"Is that you, Cal? Jude?"

No weary post-work moan of greeting, no cheery cry of identity. Claire drops her headphones on the back of the record sleeve, neatly framing the song titles, and stiffens at the sight.

Tonight/When You're Alone/The Dead Are Coming/For You/The Dead Beat/At Your Door/Lose Yourself in Us/Claire.

The night beyond her window has been eaten by deep swirls of featureless grey — the pane might as well be mirroring the album cover. Old stairs creak beneath six unseen feet as they approach the second floor.

Claire lunges at her bedroom door and slams it shut, catching a glimpse of tall shapes on the hallway wall, gaunt and attenuated as Nosferatu's shadow. There is no lock to throw, and her weight would not hold anything back for long.

She falls back against her bed as the record spins on, dazzling flecks flashing within like mica chips in a headstone, like colours that flicker in water as the surface recedes and the sun and sky are lost forever.

She closes her eyes and curls up into a ball as her bedroom door creaks open. A graveyard chill envelops the room.

A hand lifts her turntable arm and puts it aside. Fingers pluck the LP free and slide it back into its sleeve. Claire holds herself tight and tries hard not to exist.

It isn't long before she doesn't have to try at all.

Jude doesn't know if Claire ran off or got murdered or what, but in any case, she's not here paying her share. Seems fair, then, if Jude keeps the grey record she found on Claire's bed. Looks like some heavy *sturm und drang* — wicked!

Even better: the last song bears her name.

CONFECTIOUS

When a nurse comes down the hall, I show him the visible joins at my elbows, knees, shoulders, every joint weeping a pale putrescence — as if I'm a doll that some sullen child has stuffed with stale cream — and, fascinated, he dabs at my infection, this sickly confection, sniffs it... then licks his fingers clean and laughs, a hideous hunger swelling him, and he's all over me until my seeping hands grab a bedpan and pulp his face into sticky red jam, but he's not alone on duty tonight, and they're all laughing, licking their sweet teeth as they come.

MISERICORDIA

We caught them on the beach, and all around us they lie with limbs frozen forever in that final stride toward freedom. Now she is the last, on her knees before me as the reddening tide seeps in around us, eager to claim one more cooling heart, and I raise my blade to the indifferent sun.

Most would beg or weep or look down to the sand at the last; many have. But she stares up at me, into me, and her eyes are dry and clear. I see an entire life there, right up to this final moment: pain, perseverance, loss, joy, suffering, survival. And for the first time in my life... I hesitate.

Why? It's not beauty staying my hand — I've cut down the richest of blossoms, nipped unripe buds without a second thought, and she hasn't the classical looks that inspire verse or song. She's beautiful in an everyday sense, bearing the grace that comes of a kind heart and hands worked to the bone without a moment's complaint, and she exudes the type of strength most men will never understand or even recognise — the strength to birth us and build us, be bedded by us and bury us, even as we blind ourselves to their sacrifice with wine and wenching and war. I see this, and still wonder why I have yet to dash that beauty from her... for when I die, the path I walk will be awash with blood, and every step of the way I will be judged by the ignoble and innocent alike.

She does not blink. This once, I do. And then I feel a wave breaking within me, a high blood-tide stemmed by its own fury, and the rage that defines me — that *is* me — is gone. My sword is suddenly so heavy with the weight of its wretched work that my hand begins to tremble.

It is enough, now. A point has been made, underlined, scored deep into the sand. One more death proves nothing. We are *done*. Life goes on; let it be as it will.

But her *eyes*. So strong, so clear — there's fear there, yes, but also acceptance — a grace I cannot begin to put into words, a strength I will never know. She has waited all her years for this moment, and she is ready to embrace it. We have taken everything from her, but now she will have it all back and more, forever. In this moment, it is more than inevitable; it is *right*. There is a grim beauty to this, one it is beyond me to despoil. I would let her stand, walk away, for this one time I would not deny mercy — in this moment, I would give her anything. But I know what it is she wants most.

The blade falls, and she takes that final stride toward freedom. She was the last, and now the sea claims one more cooling heart. And with it, my own.

TORNADO GIRL

The tornado is finally done with our town, leaving a hot, wet wound wherever it went, and now we uncover our heads to count the cost.

There's a girl on our lawn. Face-down, naked, still.

I run to the kitchen window, curious. With a warning cry, Mother grabs me and hustles me away, but for a moment I see the girl again. She's got leaves tangled in her hair. Her body is a rainbow of brutal bruises. Her spine is warped, her limbs crooked. And she's waving as she stares in at me through the kitchen window, and she's smiling.

CATCHING FLIES

Jared was old enough, at ten, to know it was wrong — but he *hated* grown people.

They filled cafés with the drone of boring gossip, blocked footpaths with their painful perambulations, stared at flowers and weeds alike for minutes on end like there was anything at all to see. They constantly complained about technology, coloured people, anyone younger than themselves. His own grandparents were the worst; Jared dreaded the way they leaned in to kiss him, their slack mouths looming like stale open tombs. They'd already stopped living years ago, so why couldn't they just... *die*?

Even tonight, as he and his friends strode the streets in all their garish glory, Jared was reminded of his phobia. Plastic skeletons hung from verandahs, needing only drab dresses and grey wigs to join society; glowing pumpkins gave gap-toothed grins like old-timers with their dentures out. And the house at 47 Schumacher Street exhibited no life other than the rocking chair on its porch, forever ticking back and forth like a pendulum counting down the days until its ancient occupant finally gave up the ghost.

"This place won't have any lollies," he declared. "Or *braaaaains.*"

Jared had gone all-out with his zombie costume, but his friends had put in the bare minimum of effort. Cally wore an off-the-rack Wonder Woman outfit, Jai had wrapped himself in toilet paper to become the world's lamest mummy, and Declan, laziest of all, had simply put on one glove and declared himself Michael Jackson.

"Let's skip it, then," Cally suggested.

Jared's eyes flew to the porch of 47 where the old man rocked in his chair like every other day and night, barely even noticing as the world went by. His mouth hung open in that slack-jawed manner exclusive to the elderly, and Jared felt a bright blade of hatred pierce his heart.

"Nah. We get heaps of treats. Let's play a trick."

Jared explained his plan. They stashed their lolly sacks behind the fence of 45 — home to Doctor Chisholm, who never handed out candy but only gazed speculatively at young trick-or-treaters — and snuck into 47's yard. They weren't as quiet as Jared would've liked, given the rustle of Jai's bog-roll bandages, but the chatter of passing children masked their progress, and unkempt trees hid them from the porch. Soon they were through the overgrown garden and crouching at the corner of the house, holding in giggles.

"Me first," Jared whispered. "The old dude's gonna crap his pants!"

Declan grinned, but Cally and Jai looked uncomfortable. Maybe they'd had the same thought as Jared: one good, sudden fright might be enough to inconvenience the geezer in a more permanent manner. The difference? Jared didn't care.

A set of steps allowed him access to the porch from the side. Boards creaked, but the codger must have been nearly deaf; he rocked on, blissfully unaware of the impending shock.

Jared hunched low, swallowed a nervous laugh, and then

sprang across the porch with an unearthly wail and landed right beside the old dude, fingers contorted into claws, fake blood bubbling on his lips.

The rocking chair came to an abrupt halt, and that was all.

Until the pensioner slowly turned his head.

Up close, Jared saw that the man's eyes were dull and glassy, old marbles pushed into rotting meat. The dude *reeked*. His mouth still hung open in a parody of shock, but as Jared watched, aghast, a fat black fly spiralled out of it. And then another. And another.

A scream exploded behind him, and Jared flinched even as he realised it was only Declan, following his lead. Too late. His bowels loosened in a thunderclap heartbeat, and the flies pouring from the old man's mouth knew it. As his friends fled shrieking with laughter, Jared stuck to the spot, shamed and stinking – unable to move even as the old man loomed over the arm of his rocking chair, that gaping mouth breathless and buzzing, and leaned in for his Halloween kiss.

HACKLES

Doctor Chisholm had slipped halfway out of wakefulness in his favourite armchair, one hand cradling a glass of single malt, the other dangling over the edge to rest on Mercury's warm back. Now he snapped into full awareness, Mercury tensing under his fingers and raising his hackles. An unwelcome sound echoed in the back of his mind, the brutal splintering of wood — not from a dream, but nearby.

"Easy, boy," he whispered, but Mercury had risen to his feet, huffing in disquiet. Whoever had forced the back door was inside now, not bothering to hide their presence — two voices, a low, hard hum of conversation pulsing like a foreign heartbeat from the rear of the house. Mercury growled low in his throat and clicked long nails on the floorboards.

Chisholm could have kicked himself for not being prepared. Now, it appeared, someone might gladly relieve him of that burden. He glanced around the den, woozy from the scotch, his eyes cutting from one potential weapon to the next. Fountain pen? Not very daunting. Walking stick? If this was a movie and it had a sword inside, maybe; he made a mental note to look into that later, along with sturdier locks for the back door. Dog bowl? Sure, give the intruders something to laugh at as they were beating him to a pulp.

The voices were close now. Mercury bared his teeth and made to rush the door barking, but Chisholm hissed and ushered him back behind the armchair. He couldn't risk involving his pet — given the nature of this intrusion, violence was inevitable, and he still hadn't laid his hands on anything that might even the odds. Umbrella? Don't be an idiot. Scalpel? Ah, now.

He was standing in the centre of the den when the door flew open and the interlopers were revealed.

Chisholm knew them both, though not well. Parker's troubled young son Frederick had once been a patient, though it'd been only the mother who sat outside as Chisholm went about his business; the other man was Caldwell, a family friend. Both were dressed in black and expressions of stern resolution. Parker was wielding the crowbar he'd used to jemmy the back door, whilst Caldwell's fingers flexed around a cricket bat. They'd brought a third, unseen friend with them: idiot violence.

"What the hell d'you think you're doing? Get out of my house at once!"

Parker scowled. "Where is he? Where's Freddie?"

"How should I know where your neglected child has gotten to — and furthermore, why do you seem to care now?"

His face reddening, Parker stepped forward, brandishing the crowbar. "No more smart words, Doctor. *Where's my son?*"

A growl rose from the shadows around the armchair. Before Parker could do more than look, Mercury shot from his crouch on the floor and pounced upon the intruder. His teeth found the flesh of Parker's cheek, his legs scrabbling at the man's belly as they fell screaming and howling to the floor.

Caldwell stood rooted to the spot, his face frozen in horror, and Chisholm took the opportunity to move.

"No!" Parker screamed, as Mercury's spit-slicked teeth found his throat. "Please! Freddie, what are you —"

His pleas ended in a wet gurgle. Caldwell took up the chorus now, screaming as blood flecked the floorboards, but only until Chisholm slashed the scalpel across his throat. The doctor danced back to avoid the arterial spray, clinically detached as Caldwell spasmed and choked and finally lay still.

"Good boy," he whispered, and Mercury padded over to lick his bloody hand. "This is your home now. They've had their trick; time for your treat."

Mercury sat on his haunches and licked his chops as Chisholm went to work with the scalpel, waiting patiently for his bone. Tomorrow, the doctor thought, he'd buy heavy new locks for the back door — and why not look into the cost of a walking stick with a sword hidden inside, like the movies? After tonight, he deserved a treat, too.

WHAT I DID ON THE WEEKEND BY TAYLOR CASSIDY, CLASS 2A

My Mummys a vampire and she kept taking my blood so last night I kilt her.

I know what vampire's are because of I seen them everywhere, on my friends DVD's and on poster's in the mall and stuff. I always wandered why my Mummy slept all day in a dark room but I never until a few week's ago worked out why. Then I knew she was a vampire and vampire's are curst so I knew I'd be helping her, if I kilt her. I couldnt chop her head off because Im too small and that would also be mean to Mummy. And we didn't have any stake's except the one's in the refridgitater but that would be silly, so I had to use a knife and that worked. But it took a long time and Mummy woked up and she cryed and so I cryed to and, then she stopped.

Aunty Karen I think is going to be mad at me when I get home. Aunty Karen come's to make me lunch's and stuff but she isn't my real Aunty, but she is really nice. Aunty Karen saids that Mummy needed my blood to make her better because, the doctor they have saids my blood was the only good blood for her. And they saids that Mummy had her own vampire which was getting her which was called a Neemia.

And that was why she had all the tube's and, some times they had to put a ouchy big needle in me and take my blood out and give it to her. Well she's safe now and Im happy the Neemia cant get her blood anymore and make her have to take my blood.

Its OK, because Ive got it all back now.

OF COLDEST COAL

You better be good for once, her father had said after tucking her in, *it's never too late to cancel Christmas*, and Cayce knew this was the worst time to misbehave — but it was five in the morning, and six presents were waiting for her under the tree, and she'd never make it to unwrapping time at seven without at least one little peek.

Easing open her bedroom door, Cayce mentally warned Edgar not to give her away. Edgar was her imaginary friend, but it was okay because Cayce *knew* he wasn't real. He was a "passing phase", a "projection". She was nine, not stupid.

The eerie pre-dawn silence made Cayce think of her house as a grave, and of herself as the worm that wriggled through it — through the rotten heart of the apple that was her parents' happiness. She dare not wake them now and add yet another infringement to her long list of transgressions. It was entirely possible they were just one rage away from selling her to a circus or dumping her in an asylum. So why was she being bad, *again*?

Because — the presents.

Here they were, in a living room bleached empty and

soulless by a faint light the colour of dirty dishwater that seeped in around the curtains. Cayce crept straight to the tree that loomed crooked and ugly in the gloom, picked up her first present. The loose wrapping paper fell apart in her hands, and when she saw what lay within, she couldn't help but tear through the rest of her gifts in frantic disbelief.

She sat back, swallowing a bitter sob.

Each present contained nothing but a lump of cold black coal.

Her parents had *known* she would creep out here early, had set her this ghastly trap. Their hot anger was terrible, but this cold judgement was far worse. *Why couldn't she ever do anything right?*

In the lifting grey gloom, she spied two large cards, rough-hewn by clumsy child-hands and given names by a coarse crayon scrawl. One card was for CAYCE. The other —

She blinked, stupefied. The second card was for EDGAR.

With an ill ripple of dread, she reached forward with coal-smudged hands and opened it.

Merry Christmas! was written on one side, a crude but detailed picture drawn on the other in vibrant shades of red, yellow, pink, green. A boy danced beneath a joyful and jagged tree, his smile wide and cruel in victory, holding the hands of two adults. The happiness in those roughly sketched faces as they beheld the boy was something Cayce had never seen when they looked at *her*.

With a sick twinge of anticipation, she opened the card marked CAYCE.

Merry Christmas! was written and then gleefully X'd out on one side, a crude but terrifying picture drawn on the other in shades of black, grey, darker black. A girl cringed under a crooked and ugly tree, her mouth turned upside-down, shying away from the sooty hands of two adults. Six unwrapped ebon lumps surrounded her feet. Another four had been scribbled in the eye sockets of the parent-things, and tear-trails ran like mascara from their dead black stares.

Cayce jumped up as more of the lifeless lounge was revealed by the dirty glow that was too grey and washed-out to be sunlight. The carpet was filthy, the walls smudged with countless black marks; she thought now not of a grave, but a cell.

Everything was wrong, or perhaps it was just her, wrong *again* and *again* and *always*. She turned to flee back to her room, and finally saw the slump-shouldered figures that had been standing in the shadowed corners of the lounge all along. She couldn't bring herself to think of them as her parents, even though she knew those tear-streaked faces so well, and she couldn't bring herself to look away, even as they lifted heavy heads and raised long-fingered sooty hands and stared right through her with eyes of coldest coal.

SOFTLY THROUGH THE SHADOWS

Hours after the lights went out, Robert lay restless and regretted his appetite, his belly distended and sickly from the trick-or-treating spoils he'd devoured. His bed, usually as warm and welcoming as his mother's arms, held him like a queasy stomach that refused to accept its squirming contents.

Scant moonlight recast his colourful bedroom as a dim cell of unseen terrors, biding their time until they were ready to spring. His Halloween costume hung from a coathanger on the curtain rod, and for all that he'd made it with his own hands, the thing gave him a pang of discomfort. His teacher had suggested the class customise their costumes to represent something they found *scary*, rather than settling for off-the-rack replicas of mass-media superheroes. Accordingly, Robert had allowed his night terrors to take shape under trembling fingers.

The impossible creature dangling two metres away looked flat and starved without its creator inside that white-sheet body, its clown-mask face slack and lifeless, four newspaper-stuffed stockings hanging limp now the wire frames within had crumpled under the burden of pretending to be spider-legs... and yet, Robert couldn't help but imagine it was gaining solidity in the near-dark, slowly filling out, coming to life. But it was fake; he'd made it himself in an attempt to represent, to control, the thing that *really* scared him.

For though the costume disturbed him, it was the closet his eyes kept returning to—the darker-than-dark crack down the edge of the door that always seemed to creep ajar no matter how tightly he closed it. He tried to resist his unease—geez, he was ten, way too old for this!—yet a deep part of him insisted all was not well behind that door, and never mind that his parents had shown him time and again that nothing lurked within. Even when they did, his unworn clothes hung like skins torn from luckless boys, and there lurked a sense of emptiness, a mindless hunger. Whatever waited in the closet at night wanted to be filled, biding its time until its need could no longer be restrained.

And tonight was Halloween. What better time for the uncanny to creep out through the crack and gobble up the unwary? It must be after midnight by now, and Halloween was done for another year. But deep down he knew the night accepted no such man-made distinctions; once it fell, it was upon them until the dawn sent it back to the other side of the world. The darkness lingered like a growing appetite, and every minute edged the closet door a little further open.

He told himself to think like his parents and understand this was simply his imagination. The dread in his roiling, sweet-stuffed belly begged to differ.

Robert turned again to the costume, certain it looked more substantial than last time he'd checked. But he'd created it—he controlled it. He turned away, rolled onto his back. The closet door stood further open.

He wasn't imagining it this time. Just a moment ago, that crack of black had been maybe two inches wide. Now, at least four.

Robert squeezed his eyes shut and wished for the safety of sleep, where the monsters couldn't touch him. He wished he were more grown-up, so the monsters wouldn't be believed. The door didn't hang properly, that was why it wouldn't stay shut. *Of course* it would swing wider under the steady influence of gravity. He opened his eyes.

Six inches.

A quiet screech, metal on metal. A coathanger on a steel rod.

Robert watched, paralysed, as the closet door swung silently open until it stood parallel to the dark mouth it revealed. Clothes rustled like whispering witnesses and parted to allow something through.

His bladder let go as a tall figure slunk into his bedroom, hands raised as if feeling the air. The creature was as white as his costume, like something that had only ever lived in a cave or at the bottom of the lightless ocean. He closed his eyes, praying it would leave him alone if it thought him asleep. Perhaps it visited him every night and never touched him for just that reason. But he couldn't bear that it was right there and unseen, so his eyes snapped open again. The thing was alongside his bed now, shuffling ever closer.

Another metallic squeak, like a coathanger swaying in the breeze, only there was no movement in the room besides the approaching ghoul.

Until Robert's Halloween costume dropped from its wire-frame noose and sprang forward, its sagging mouth full of teeth that no longer resembled plastic vampire fangs, wrapping its spider-legs around the intruder and bearing it to the floor.

Robert lay still as the wet sheets cooled around him, staring in shock at the ceiling as the horrid sounds of feeding went on and on.

He couldn't move. He *had* to move. If he was ever so

quiet, he could slip out of bed and out of his room while the thing was distracted. As slowly as the moon arced across the sky, he folded back his sheets, drew his legs up, rose to a sitting position. Without looking at the grim feast just feet away, he tensed himself to spring off the bed.

A spider-leg curled around his upper arm, soft and slick and utterly unlike the old stocking it had been before the bedroom light went out.

His throat locked shut. Robert froze as the leg dragged him to the end of his bed. His feet hit the carpet, and the ghastly grip went away. Before he could flee, he was shoved into the darkness of his closet. The door shut behind him. This time, it had no trouble staying closed.

Robert waited, shivering in the dark. After a long time, he fell forward onto his hands and knees. The surface beneath him was cold, unforgiving—no trace of the carpet, his shoes, or the clothes that should have been hanging around him. He turned and saw nothing, turned again, nothing. He was lost in a pitch-black void, his senses nulled.

Eventually, he rose and began to walk.

Seconds bled into years as time lost all meaning. He wanted to believe he was still in bed, dreaming, but he could no longer convince himself this was true.

Onward he went, numb and chill, for what might have been forever. Over time, his pyjamas split and rotted from his growing body, leaving his pallid flesh exposed to the dark. His hair and teeth fell out until he was smooth, soft, alien to his own touch. And all the while, as he walked on and on through the boundless black, his hunger grew. A pang became a yearning, a constant, gnawing agony in his belly. The abyss ate his memories until he could no longer recall where he'd come from, who he'd known, even his own name.

Forever had gone well beyond unbearable when his fingers brushed something for the first time in his corrupted memory.

Confused, he touched the skins hanging before him, hides nothing like his own rotten-apple flesh, and remembered he had eyes when he saw a vertical line of dim light splitting the darkness ahead. Unknown, unnamed emotions returned to him, and he reached out to this revelation.

He left the darkness that was all he knew and found himself in a place he could barely understand. The ground was soft and furry, and *things* stood all around in the confined space, things he felt he should remember but could not. A long, rectangular object sat before him—a small creature was folded within its depths, staring at him with eyes wide and fearful. He felt he should know this beast, that it should know him. He was just as terrified as this strange being seemed to be, but he stumbled forward, hands clutching at the hope of release, ignoring the pale, empty shape that hung nearby. The agony in his stomach reached a crescendo that sounded like a metallic screech, and he knew that finally a raging appetite would be fulfilled.

INTROSPECTRE

A soul is the sum of its memories. Therefore, you are an equation. You may be proven, solved, through the application of formulae and logic.

Find the value of x, given that $x + y = z$ and $z = $ you. Show working out.

$x = $ *Laura.* The wittiest girl in class, skinny and self-conscious, always talking breathlessly about books as if to distract attention from herself. Naked below you on her parents' living room floor, intense teenage heat trapped beneath the shared blanket, an heirloom ormolu clock counting off each ecstatic moment, a gasp of enlightenment at her introduction to the sacred and profane, seventeen ticks of the clock between her gasp and yours.

(You remember no home, no family, no employment in any endeavour other than seduction.)

x = Daniel. The new barman in that trendy seaside bar, the charming novelty of his Liverpudlian accent, a U2 fanatic, knowing smiles over each foaming glass. Restricted thrashings in the back of his Daihatsu, windows cracked to stop them misting, the sea's salty scent underlaid by the coarser musk of his sweat and come, wet skin-shine below the gibbous moon.

> (Whenever you're required to give a name, which is often, you pull one at random from the lottery in your mind, not ever knowing if perhaps this one is the truth.)

x = Indigo. The goth, kohl-rimmed eyes and massive boots, the flash of playful eyes across a dark club, supple sorceress moves atop stomping beats. Fishnets tearing beneath eager fingers, razor chopping speed on her shaved pubis, nostrils burning as you plunge your tongue deep, frantic night blazing away into ashen morning, poached eggs and toast before you leave.

> (You feel a certain sense of gratitude to these fleeting partners, but the *love* of which they sometimes speak is foreign. You have no experience of it.)

x = Akito. The man who was a woman who looked like a girl, short ebony hair and down-soft leg hair, dead dreams of designing public parks. The polished brass of a high-class bar, a taxi to a faraway rented house, the childlike body of a man who has given birth to two sons, stories of an alienated family as if to validate your presence, his eyes squeezed tightly shut as if each thrust is an intrusion, stiff dry kisses of farewell.

> (You have done everything that can be done to and by and for a human, crossed every arbitrary boundary, fucked every

pliable inch. And yet this talk of *love* makes you feel like a knock-kneed virgin blushing in the corner.)

x = Karen. The thespian at the house party, a busty blonde claiming that actors are liars and cannot be trusted, a paler band of skin around her left ring finger, the quandary of a script that calls for full-frontal nudity. The taste of Baileys passing from her mouth to yours, excited fumblings in a spare bedroom, the maddening tricks of her tongue and lips, your wetness shining on her chin, shared grins across a crowded and unsuspecting patio.

(Whatever it is these constant casual companions give you, it is your sustenance — is your purpose. You are never without them, as you have nothing else.)

x = Joanna. The library assistant, creamy white skin and pinned-up crimson locks, eyes sparkling behind fashionable spectacles, flirting over discussions of Atwood and Tsiolkas. Hiding in the toilets until closing time, pressing her down on the reading table, her cries of *oh fuck oh fuck oh fuck yes*, the entrancing parabolas of her breasts counterpointing your ribald rhythms, the rich red river of hair splayed across the table behind her skull like the spray of blood from a headshot.

(You cannot be sure if you are haunting or haunted.)

x = Jessie. The middle-aged party animal, cigarette-roughened voice and saucy laugh, long bottle-blonde hair, bawling along to "Jesse's Girl" as if it's both for and about her alone. Hard and fast behind the bottle shop, tasting yourself in her mouth, the pierced clitoris and unexplained tattoo of NICKY, the rough caress of concrete on eager knees, rasping gasps of *come on fuck the shit outta me.*

(Are you dreaming this endless string of encounters, or are they dreaming you?)

$x = $ *Abimbola.* The cynical literary youth smoking a joint at the bus stop, fashionable high fade cut and nonchalantly untucked shirt, paperback poetry poking from a pocket, proud of his footballer brother. Cloistered in a toilet cubicle at the nearby park, his untrimmed cock proving the cliché, the shock of sudden blood on the condom, awkwardness and regret blooming in his wide dark eyes.

From this we may assume that $y = $ sex.

What have you learned about yourself from all this?

Nothing. Nothing is there, no matter how hard you look. You cannot see your own face, and when someone says *tell me about yourself*, there is this —

I'm Nicky the librarian and I love U2. I'm an actor and you can't trust actors, we're all liars for money. I'm Jesse, I want to design parks. My brother is a professional footballer. You can call me Laura. I drink Baileys — what's yours?

Never the same story twice, and never a true answer to be found. x is variable, therefore z is not a constant. This equation cannot be solved by half-remembered mathematics.

So what are you, then?

A vampire, feeding on meaty memories.

A ghost, haunted by the lusts of the living.

A mirror, reflecting the world's foibles and fantasies.

A sentient cluster of acquired knowledge, with nothing to truly call your own.

A monster, a meme, a dream — all valid theories.

Outside of seduction, you recall nothing, as if there is

naught else but false charm and empty talk and endless sex that leaves you a spectral echo in the mind of the fucked, a wet dream that may or may not have come true.

If unobserved, do you even exist at all?

If I smash this mirror, is this room then empty?

PLEASE STAY

Coleman was indescribably glad that Tithorea Grace had been laid to rest in a crypt — even his fanaticism might have been deterred if he'd had to dig up six feet of turf to get to her bones. But her son was famous and his singing career had borne fat fruit, so here was Coleman on Halloween night, standing in a graveyard with just a single door between the ultimate fan and the ultimate rarity.

Taking a deep breath, Coleman placed his shuttered lantern on the earth before the huddled stone crypt and examined the marble plaque to one side of the door. The simple epitaph her son had chosen was curious: *PLEASE REST IN PEACE*. Coleman shrugged it off as the eccentricity of the rich and creative, and set to work on the iron latch with his crowbar. A twisted oak tree alongside the crypt rustled at him as if in warning, but he was resolved to do this dark thing — because he, unlike most of Arcas Grace's devotees, understood that *fan* was short for *fanatic*.

The latch was weighty, unwilling to budge; obviously Arcas had never intended to visit his mother's remains. Coleman could understand why. Apart from the rumours that she'd somehow influenced his career and brought him the fame he'd wanted to earn for himself, excerpts from certain interviews hinted at a schism between Arcas and Tithorea, implied that he'd broken free from a path she'd chosen for him and made his own way in the world. Coleman thought of his own mother, eternally disappointed, and leaned harder on the crowbar until the latch gave with an indignant screech. The heavy door ground back beneath his eager shove, and he was in.

The lantern illuminated a small stone space perhaps a dozen feet square. The walls piqued Coleman's curiosity further, inscribed as they were with text in an ancient language he couldn't recognise and symbols that meant nothing to him, but similar things adorned the sleeves of Arcas Grace's debut album *Leaving the Wild Wood* — such esotericism added depth to the singer's obvious appeal. The walls themselves were not so thick as to be impregnable, however, as thick and ropy roots from the oak tree outside had forced themselves in and crept from widening cracks to the rich wood of the coffin that rested on a low dais at the centre of the crypt. But Coleman spared them little attention, as his eyes flew to the lid of the coffin and found the Grail he sought.

Like many Grails he'd seen depicted, this one was unassuming — merely a CD-R in a clear plastic case, a date marked on the disc in thick black pen. But that date had taken on a weighty significance to Coleman and his fellow followers, because on it, Arcas had played a very special show to a very select audience. It was the day after Tithorea Grace's death, and the gig had evidently meant a lot to him, for he'd insisted that all invited attendants leave their phones and cameras outside. A desk tape of the show had been recorded by Arcas's soundman, and this singular document of the performance had been laid to rest along with his mother's remains without ever being played. Most importantly, Arcas had written and recited a song especially for the occasion, one that he claimed would never be heard again — so this disc held not just the only recording of a very special gig, but the only recording of Arcas's farewell to his mother. As such, "Please Stay" was the ultimate bootleg... and now, the ultimate fan was about to take possession of it.

Coleman crept across the chamber as if leery of waking its sole occupant, his eyes locked on the CD-R. He half-expected it to bear the weight of its worth, but the case was as light and ordinary as any other when he picked it up. That mundanity, as well as awareness of his highly illegal position, caused Coleman to tuck the disc hurriedly into his pocket. The deed was done. Time to go home and revel in the spoils of this outrageous expedition.

He almost tripped over one of the roots as he turned to leave. The gnarled fingers had crept right to the wood of the coffin itself and, he fancied in the gloom, might well have been absorbed into the casket itself, since now he could see no end to them. The tree from which they extended must have been nudged by the gentle breeze again, for he heard another dry rustle. The acoustics of the crypt made him think for a moment that the sound had come from within the coffin.

Coleman pulled the door to behind him, resigned to leaving a clear sign of his intrusion. He shuttered the lantern and stowed the crowbar in his pack, remembering that he'd parked down the side of the cemetery and was only minutes from his car and freedom. Once home, he'd dim the lights and light some candles and pour himself a neat Scotch — such a hallowed night called for ritual, and "Please Stay" deserved the utmost ceremony. He transferred the CD-R from his pocket to his pack lest it somehow slip free and undo all his hard work, and another rustle hissed at him from alongside the crypt. But this one sounded almost like words uttered with hateful glee.

Distracted from his anticipation for a moment, Coleman turned and saw the ugly oak tree looming forward around the side of the low stone barrow. He'd just realised there was scarcely breeze enough to cause such a disturbance of its limbs when those long branches lashed out and hard, brittle fingers caught at his clothes. A number of revelations struck him then, but the one that screamed foremost in his mind as the oak's many arms dragged him swiftly toward its body was that the jagged hole now opening up in that gnarled wooden trunk looked very much like a mouth.

ABOUT THE AUTHOR

Matthew R. Davis is an author and musician based in Adelaide, South Australia, with over seventy short stories published around the world to date. He's been shortlisted for the Shirley Jackson, Aurealis, Australian Shadows, and Washington Science Fiction Association Small Press Awards, winning two Shadows in 2019 – the only author other than Kaaron Warren to receive two in the same year. His books include *Supermassive Black Mass* (novelette, 2019), *If Only Tonight We Could Sleep* (horror stories, 2020), *Midnight in the Chapel of Love* (novel, 2021), and *The Dark Matter of Natasha* (novella, 2022), with more on the way.

He's been writing, recording, and performing music for

many years, supporting international acts and touring interstate, appearing on a slew of albums, EPs, and singles; he is/was/may be the bassist and vocalist for eclectic heavy rockers Blood Red Renaissance and pensive prog metallers icecocoon. He's also created album and poster art for these bands, singer/songwriter Ethan Davis, and some reading events. He's been involved in many independent film projects as writer, director, editor, producer, composer, grip, and/or actor, most recently working as an extra on the local trashploitation flick *Ribspreader,* and sometimes performs spoken word with punk poets Paroxysm Press. He lives in Somerton Park and shares his life with photographer Meg Wright (aka Red Wallflower Photography).

CREDITS

"Colours That Flicker in Water" first appeared in *Petrified Punks*, Oscillate Wildly Press, 2018.

"You've Seen the Butcher" is original to this collection.

"Christmas Presence" first appeared in *Hell's Bells*, Australian Horror Writers Association, 2016.

"Confectious" first appeared in *Trembling with Fear: Year One*, The Horror Tree, 2018.

"What I Did on the Weekend by Taylor Cassidy, Class 2A" first appeared in *Robbed of Sleep 5*, Robbed of Sleep, 2016.

"Misericordia" first appeared in *The Sirens Call #18*, Sirens Call Publications, 2015.

"Tornado Girl" first appeared in *22 More Quick Shivers*, The Daily Nightmare, 2014.

"Hackles" first appeared in *Trickster's Treats #1*, Things in the Well, 2017.

"Catching Flies" first appeared in *Trickster's Treats #1*, Things in the Well, 2017.

"Of Coldest Coal" first appeared in *Shades of Santa: Tales from the Bloody North Pole*, Things in the Well, 2017.

"Softly Through the Shadows" first appeared in *Trickster's Treats #3*, Things in the Well, 2019.

"Introspectre" is original to this collection.

"Please Stay" first appeared in *Trickster's Treats #2*, Things in the Well, 2018.

THANK YOU FOR BUYING THIS BRAIN JAR PRESS CHAPBOOK

To receive special offers, bonus content, and info on
new releases and other great reads, visit us
online at www.BrainJarPress.com